THE MAKING OF A KNIGHT

OF A KNIGHT

How Sir James
Earned His Armor

PATRICK O'BRIEN

 Charlesbridge

"I am Sir James! I have come to fight for England!" James burst into his father's room, his wooden sword slashing the air before him. He imagined he was wearing a suit of shining armor, traveling the countryside in search of adventure.

"James," said his father, "put aside your sword. I need to talk to you." His father was a wise old knight, known throughout England for his bravery and strength.

"Now that you are seven years old, it is time for you to become a page in a great castle," James's father told him. "That means that one day, if you learn well and practice hard, you will become a knight, as I am. Then you will have real weapons and armor and will no longer need your sword of wood."

One summer evening soon afterward, James's mother packed his belongings in a large woolen sack. Just before going to bed, James opened the sack and carefully hid his wooden sword inside. The next morning James and his parents set off on horseback for the castle of Lord Hawkes. James had heard stories of this rich and powerful man, and now that he was going to live in his castle, he was both excited . . . and a bit scared.

On their journey James's family passed through many small villages, all of which were on land owned by Lord Hawkes. The people who lived in these villages received his protection. In return Lord Hawkes demanded a large part of their crops, their animals, and even the honey from their beehives.

Upon the recommendation of James's father, Lord Hawkes made James a page in his castle. James was now on his way to becoming a knight. During his training, he learned to play music, read, and write. With the other pages of the castle, he practiced wrestling, archery, sword fighting, and horsemanship. He and the other pages also served at the table during meals.

In James's time, there was a book about good manners written especially for pages. It was called *The Babees' Book*. By reading it, James learned how to be polite and considerate: "Do not claw at your flesh or lean against a post in the presence of your lord"; "Whether you spit near or far, hold your hand before your mouth to hide it"; and "Keep from picking your nose, your teeth, or your nails at mealtime."

One day James was practicing archery with the other pages when suddenly he heard a loud trumpet blast. Someone shouted, "The king approaches!" As the pages watched, the king of England rode slowly toward the castle on his stately charger, accompanied by the queen and an escort of nobles, servants, and soldiers. The castle's servants quickly hung large, colorful banners from the tops of the walls. With a clatter of hooves and a blare of trumpets, the royal procession rode into the courtyard to the cheers of the crowd.

Later that day a grand feast was held in honor of the king. The cooks prepared their fanciest, most exotic dishes. The guests ate from wooden plates shared between two people. No one in England used forks in those days, so the guests ate with a knife, a spoon, and their fingers. James and the other pages of the castle served the meal. They also carried a bowl of water and a towel so that the guests could wash their hands between courses.

The dogs got to eat the scraps.

This "pie" came with dessert. Small live birds were put in a pie tin and covered with a cooked pie crust. When the pie was cut open at the table, the birds flew out in a cloud of flour and feathers.

Inspired by the king's noble knights, James was more determined than ever to make his dream of knighthood come true. When no one was looking, he liked to explore the armor closet.

After the king's departure, life in the castle returned to normal. As the years passed, James continued his training, which included learning chivalry from the ladies of the castle. Chivalry was a system of beliefs about how a knight should act. Lady Allison often said, "A chivalrous knight is honorable, truthful, and loyal. He is kind and generous to anyone in need, and he is always merciful and fair, even to his enemies." A knight was also courteous and gentle toward the ladies. If he liked a particular lady and wanted to win her heart, he composed poems and songs of love for her. He also performed brave deeds in her honor.

On James's fourteenth birthday, Lord Hawkes said to him, "Congratulations, James. You have learned well, and today you will be made a squire. Well done." This was the next step toward knighthood. As a squire, James would serve a knight of the castle, caring for his weapons and armor and doing chores for him. He would even sleep beside the knight's bed at night.

James was made a squire to a brave and powerful knight named Sir Thomas of Hammersmith. At first James was a little afraid of Sir Thomas, who at times could be gruff and intimidating. However, the knight was very kind in his own way. "If you pay attention to all I have to teach you," said Sir Thomas, "you will become a great knight like your father . . . and like me."

One of James's duties as squire was to care for Sir Thomas's horses. A knight had several horses, and each was used for a different purpose.

Sir Thomas had a large, strong horse that he rode in battle.

This is the horse Sir Thomas used for jousting. It was a powerful horse called a destrier.

Sir Thomas also had a fast horse called a courser.

The palfrey was a well-mannered, easy-paced horse that Sir Thomas used for traveling. The sumpter was only used to carry baggage.

James also learned about the art of falconry, or hawking. The nobles of the castle used trained falcons, a type of hawk, to hunt for small animals and birds. The nobles dressed in their finest clothes and sometimes went out for several days on horseback. When game was spotted, a falcon was released. It swooped down, caught its prey, and then brought it back to the hunters. Many nobles treated their favorite falcon as a pet and carried the bird around on their arm when they went visiting.

A leather hood was placed on the falcon's head. This kept it calm until the moment of the hunt, when the hood was removed.

James made friends with this puppy on a hunt and named him Cedrick. From then on, James always had Cedrick at his side.

"James, the armorer has finished making my new helmet," said Sir Thomas one day. "I need you to fetch it for me."

Inside the hot, noisy armorer's workshop, several craftsmen were hammering and bending sheets of metal, shaping the various pieces of a suit of armor. The armorer explained to James, "Each suit of armor is specially made to fit a different knight, and I know the size of every piece for each knight in the castle!" Different types of armor had to be made for various activities: battle armor for wartime, jousting armor for tournaments, and parade armor just for showing off.

This is what knights wore in the 1200s, about two hundred years before James was born. There were no metal plates, but knights were fairly well protected by a suit of mail that was made of thousands of small, interlocking metal rings.

By the 1400s, in James's time, knights were entirely covered by metal. These suits of armor usually weighed about sixty pounds, but were easier to move around in than you might think. They could get hot and uncomfortable, though, especially on a long ride in the summertime.

This pig-faced basinet was used in battle.

This is a frog-mouthed helm. It was only used for jousting.

This kind of helmet was only used for show.

As a squire, James had to keep Sir Thomas's weapons in perfect shape. He also began to acquire his own. Mastering them was difficult, but necessary. As a knight, James's life would depend on his skill.

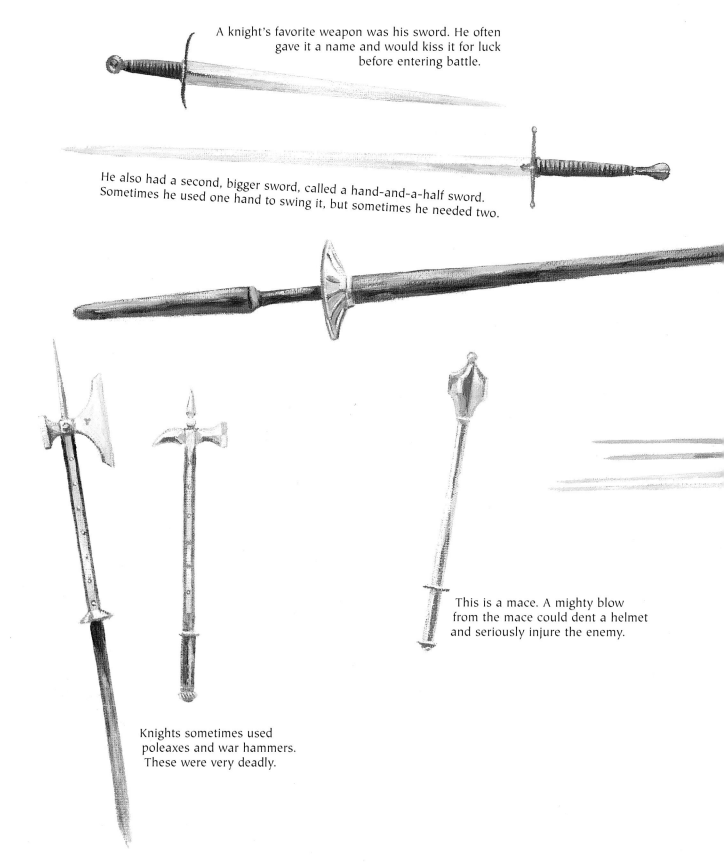

A knight's favorite weapon was his sword. He often gave it a name and would kiss it for luck before entering battle.

He also had a second, bigger sword, called a hand-and-a-half sword. Sometimes he used one hand to swing it, but sometimes he needed two.

This is a mace. A mighty blow from the mace could dent a helmet and seriously injure the enemy.

Knights sometimes used poleaxes and war hammers. These were very deadly.

This is a lance. The knight held it out in front of him while charging another knight on horseback. The lance knocked the enemy off his horse, perhaps even piercing his armor and killing him.

James was now nineteen and close to knighthood. He had learned much, but he had yet to experience a real battle. James's chance came one summer morning when a band of enemy knights appeared on the horizon. The castle's heavy iron gates creaked open, and a colorful procession of armored knights and their squires rode out to meet the enemy.

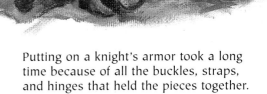

Putting on a knight's armor took a long time because of all the buckles, straps, and hinges that held the pieces together.

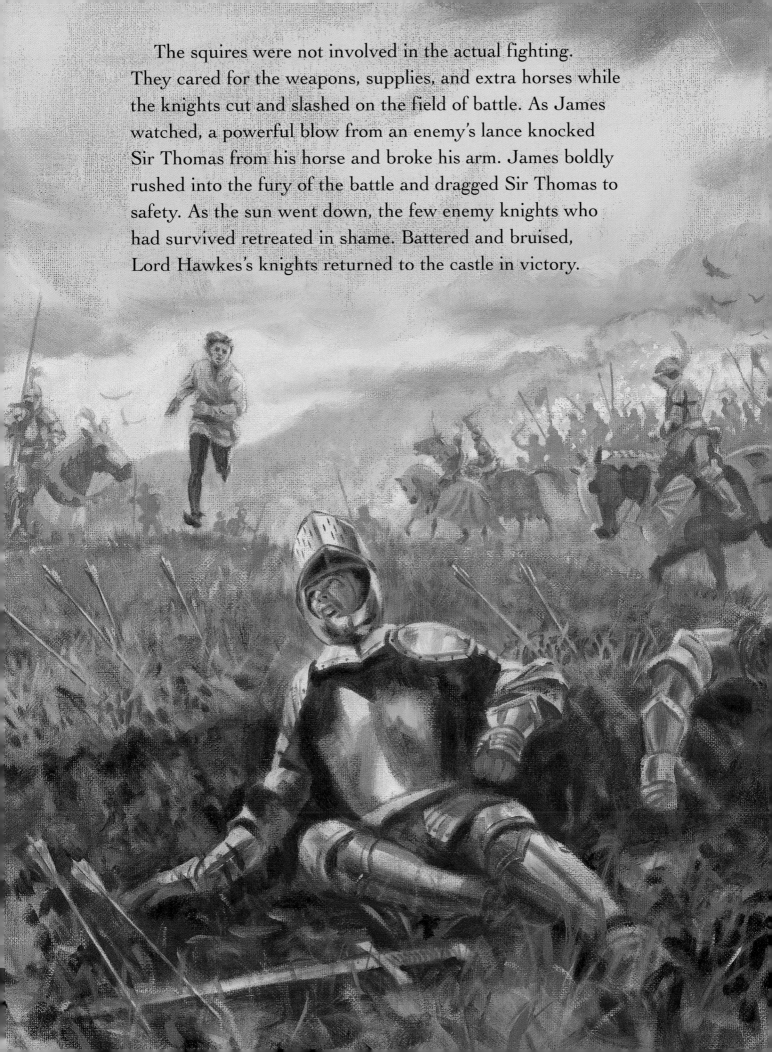

The squires were not involved in the actual fighting. They cared for the weapons, supplies, and extra horses while the knights cut and slashed on the field of battle. As James watched, a powerful blow from an enemy's lance knocked Sir Thomas from his horse and broke his arm. James boldly rushed into the fury of the battle and dragged Sir Thomas to safety. As the sun went down, the few enemy knights who had survived retreated in shame. Battered and bruised, Lord Hawkes's knights returned to the castle in victory.

At last, when James turned twenty-one, he was ready to be knighted. He was careful to follow the traditional rituals before the ceremony. First he had a long bath to symbolically cleanse his soul, and then he shaved his beard and cut his hair. He spent the night in a church, thinking about the responsibilities of knighthood.

In the morning he entered the great hall, where a large crowd was gathered. His proud mother and father were standing right in front. Lord Hawkes made James a knight by lightly striking him on the shoulder with a sword, saying, "I dub thee knight. Be loyal, brave, and true." Then Lord and Lady Hawkes strapped James's sword and belt on his waist and buckled golden spurs to his ankles. He was now Sir James, the newest knight in the castle.

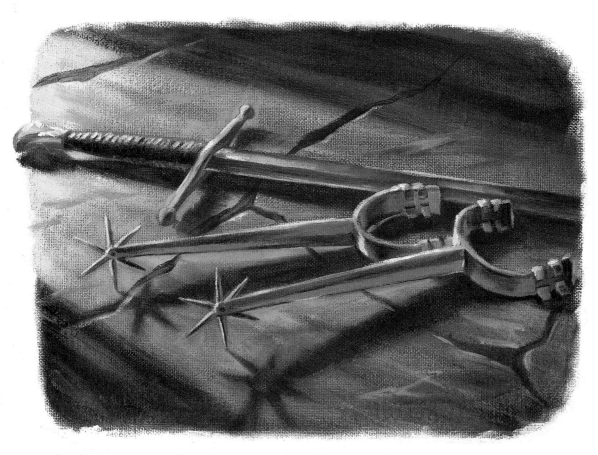

A knight wore spurs on his ankles to help control his horses. He was very proud of them because they were a symbol of his noble status.

Sir James was just getting used to his new armor when a traveling knight approached the castle gates. "If there is any knight in the castle who is brave of heart and strong of arm, let him come forth and joust with me," he challenged. Sir James rushed for his lance and armor and rode out to meet the challenger.

In a grassy field outside the castle, a small crowd gathered to watch Sir James and the other knight as they charged at each other. With a mighty crash, Sir James splintered his stout lance against the other's shield. With new lances, they lined up again and charged. This time Sir James was knocked roughly to the ground.

Sir James had lost the joust. According to the rules, he had to give his armor and horse to the winner. But as a gesture of chivalry, the victorious knight refused to accept them, saying, "Keep them, young knight. It seems your need for them is greater than my own."

Sir James had noticed a beautiful young noblewoman in the crowd watching the joust. Her name was Catherine, and she was new to the castle. Much taken by her beauty, Sir James began to write love poems and songs for her.

Catherine promised to return his love if he acted with chivalry and performed valiant deeds in her honor. She gave him her scarf and said, "Tie this around your arm when you joust to show that you act in my name. In this way you will win my heart."

Later that summer Lord Hawkes sent his heralds far and wide with an important announcement. A tournament would be held at the castle in the next month. This series of warlike games was held in a fenced area called the lists, where knights fought one another to show off their strength and skill. People came from miles around to watch the spectacle. The most exciting part of the tournament was the mêlée, where large groups of knights fought in teams, much like a real battle.

The mêlée was good practice for a real war. But sometimes tempers got too hot. Soon it was not just for sport anymore—it was for real.

A squire helps his defeated master.

The most important part of the tournament was the joust. Sir Everest, a famous warrior, announced, "Any knight who defeats me at the joust shall win my finest shining armor. But if he loses, I shall wear his armor at my next match." Three knights had already fallen when Sir James had his chance.

On the first charge both Sir Everest and Sir James shattered their lances. The next charge, Sir James's lance held, and Sir Everest was lifted from his horse and thrown to the ground. With Catherine's scarf waving from his arm, Sir James was declared the winner.

Now that Sir James had proven himself as a knight, he needed his own squire. There was a page at the castle named Robert who had a talent for swordplay, and Sir James made him his squire. At first Robert was a little afraid of the mighty knight who had won the joust at the tournament, but he felt honored to be his squire.

After a few years serving Lord Hawkes at the castle, Sir James decided to set off in search of adventure and fortune, becoming a knight-errant. He said good-bye to Catherine, promising to see her upon his return. As the gate of the castle creaked open, Sir James rode out proudly with Robert following closely behind. Packed deep in his bags, beneath the armor and the mail, beneath the warm coats and Catherine's scarf, was his little wooden sword. Wearing his finest suit of shining armor, Sir James rode off to a new life of adventure.

I would like to thank my brother, Charlie, and my editor, Yolanda LeRoy,
for their invaluable help with the writing of this story.
—P. O'B.

Published by Charlesbridge
85 Main Street, Watertown, MA 02472
(617) 926-0329
www.charlesbridge.com

Library of Congress Cataloging-in-Publication Data
O'Brien, Patrick, 1960–
The making of a knight: how Sir James earned his armor/Patrick O'Brien.
p. cm.
Summary: Traces James's journey during the Middle Ages in England from
inexperienced page at the age of seven to knighthood at the age of twenty-one.
ISBN 978-0-88106-354-7 (reinforced for library use)
ISBN 978-0-88106-355-4 (softcover)
ISBN 978-1-60734-326-4 (ebook pdf)
[1. Knights and knighthood—Fiction. 2. England—Social life and customs—
1066–1485—Fiction. 3. Middle Ages—Fiction.] I. Title.
PZ7.01295Mak   1998
[Fic]—dc21   97-36867

Printed in Korea
(hc) 10 9 8 7 6 5 4 3
(sc) 15 14 13

The illustrations in this book were done in oil on canvas.
The display type and text type were set in Aquitaine, Cochin, and Tiepolo.
Color separations were made by Eastern Rainbow, Derry, New Hampshire.
Printed by Sung In Printing in Gunpo-Si, Kyonggi-Do, Korea
Production supervision by Brian G. Walker
Designed by Diane M. Earley

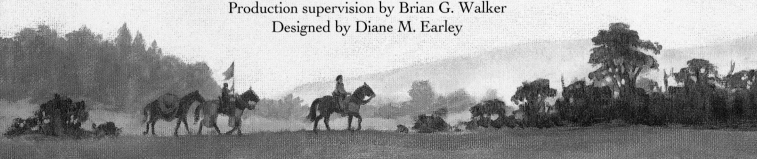